Maria Loretta Giraldo   Nicoletta Bertelle

TRY AND SAY
ABRACADABRA!

Ragged Bears

All the little birds were learning how to fly for the first time.
The first one to go was Blackbird. As she leapt off the branch she shouted "Yippee!"
Then it was Robin's turn; "Hooray!" he chirped in delight.
Next was Sparrow, who shouted, "Yay! Flying is so much fun!"

First published in 2018 by Ragged Bears Ltd
Sherborne, DT9 3PH
www.ragged-bears.co.uk

ISBN: 978 185714 4680

Written by MARIA LORETTA GIRALDO
Illustrated by NICOLETTA BERTELLE
Moral rights asserted

Original title: *Prova a dire Abracadabra*
© Camelozampa, Italy, 2017

A CIP catalogue record for this book is available from the British Library

Printed in Italy

Only Little Owl was still standing on the branch
with his wings by his side.
"Come on Little Owl, fly with us" said Mrs Pigeon,
the teacher.
"I don't want to" Little Owl whimpered.

Then along came Tortoise.
 "Hello Little Owl" she said, "Why aren't you flying
with your friends?"
"It's because I'm scared I'll fall down," said Little Owl.
"Nonsense" said Tortoise. "With a bit of practice,
you will surely succeed."
But Little Owl shook his head "No, I'll never be able
to do it!"

Tortoise thought about it and then declared;
"I know a foolproof way for being able to do things…
Try and say 'Abracadabra!' It's a super magical word.
Spread your wings and say it and you will be able to fly."
"Are you sure?"
"I'm absolutely certain."

Little Owl opened his wings and said "Abicidabra!"
And… **CRASH!** He fell to the ground.
"Ouch! Did you see that? Your magic word doesn't work at all!"
"You didn't say it properly!" Tortoise pointed out.
"You have to say **ABRACADABRA**. Try again."

Just then, Mouse turned up. "What's going on here?" he asked.
"Little Owl is afraid to fly" Tortoise explained.
"Really?" Mouse asked, "You just need to say Abracadabra...
It's a super magical word!"

Little Owl shook his head.

"It doesn't work. I just tried it and I fell down anyway."

"But you have to say it correctly," Tortoise insisted.

Little Owl went back up the tree.

He closed his eyes and said, "ABRACADABRA!"

He fluttered along a little way, and then… **CRASH!**

"Ouch ouch! But I said it right!" Little Owl cried.

"That's true, but you had your eyes shut" said Mouse.

"Try again, but this time keep your eyes open."

Little Owl climbed back up, his eyes open wide.

"Abracadabra" he said again.

He lifted off, and briefly flew a little way, and a little way further…

But then… CRASH!

"Ouch ouch ouch!" he cried out loudly.

Then Hedgehog arrived: "What's the matter here?" he asked.

"Little Owl is trying to fly" Mouse and Tortoise told him.

"Has he tried using Abracadabra? That's guaranteed to work," Hedgehog suggested.
"I have said it so many times, but I keep falling down!" complained Little Owl.
"Maybe you said it too quietly. Try shouting it with all your might!"

Little Owl clambered up again, with his eyes open and his wings outstretched. He shouted as loudly as he could: **"ABRACADABRA!"** This time, he lifted off and started to fly, Little Owl flew and flew through the air. **"Woo-hoo! It's wonderful!"**

"Goodbye my friends, and thank you for all your help!"
Little Owl looked down – he was not afraid of heights anymore.
The wind carried him to the pond where the school for baby frogs
was. It was a very important day: the young frogs were trying to
take a big leap out of the water to reach the ground.
The first frog jumped and… "Bravo!"
Then the second frog leapt into the air; "Excellent!"
Eventually most of them had jumped out.

But there was still one baby frog in the pond.

"Hey, why are you still in the pond?" Little Owl asked.

"I can't jump. I'm afraid to fall down and hurt myself!" he replied.

"Don't worry!" Little Owl said, "**Try and say Abracadabra!**
It's a super magical word! But it might not work straight away.
You must try again and again, and never lose hope, like I did."

"Are you sure?" the baby frog asked.

"Absolutely certain!" said Little Owl.